S0-APC-589

BOBBY'S

RETIREMENT HUMOR

WHAT TO DO IN RETIREMENT

CLAUDE FILION
AND DAVID GNASS

BOBBY'S

RETIREMENT HUMOR
WHAT TO DO IN RETIREMENT

CLAUDE FILLON
AND DAVID GNASS

Copyright © 2012 by Claude Filion and David Gnass.

Library of Congress Control Number: 2012907246
ISBN: Hardcover   978-1-4771-0098-1
               Softcover   978-1-4771-0097-4
               Ebook   978-1-4771-0099-8

All rights reserved. No part of this book may be reproduced or transmitted
in any form or by any means, electronic or mechanical, including photocopying,
recording, or by any information storage and retrieval system, without permission
in writing from the copyright owner.

This book was printed in the United States of America.

To order additional copies of this book, contact:
Xlibris Corporation
1-888-795-4274
www.Xlibris.com
Orders@Xlibris.com
105050

Summary of Chapters

The book is dedicated to April.

Many thanks to our family and friends, for their advice and encouragement.

Preface

This is a cartoon book featuring Bobby, a dog with ideas on how people can be active after they retire. Bobby shares his ideas with the reader. He also provides illustrations of his two masters, both retirees, performing each activity in a way that is silly or perilous to them, but humorous to the reader. The humor is witty, lighthearted and unpretentious.

About the Authors

Claude Filion resides in Ottawa, Canada, with his two dogs, Tommy and Bobby. Claude has been a lawyer since 1986. He has also given hundreds of seminars to people planning their retirement.

David Gnass resides in Kingston, Canada, with his spouse Azza, and daughter April. David has been an artist since 1990, in the medium of oil on canvas. He also draws cartoons and illustrates children's books.

Introduction

Finally, it's your last day at work. No more bosses, assignments, deadlines, or stress. Now you're retired. Jump up, and kick your heels.

CLAUDE FILION AND DAVID GNASS

Ouch! I bet that hurt. Of course, to enjoy your retirement, you should look where you're going. You should also be active. Let me give you ideas on ways to be active, starting with:

1. LEISURE ACTIVITIES

Dining

Bon appétit.

Watching Movies

Will you stop crying? The movie hasn't even started.

CLAUDE FILION AND DAVID GNASS

Driving

This is the last time I read you a bedtime story in the car.

Playing Chess

Checkmate.

CLAUDE FILION AND DAVID GNASS

Juggling

How do you like my act so far?

Playing Music

CLAUDE FILION AND DAVID GNASS

Flying Kites

I don't like the design on our kite.

Visiting Fairs

I think you made a wrong turn somewhere.

CLAUDE FILION AND DAVID GNASS

Bird-Watching

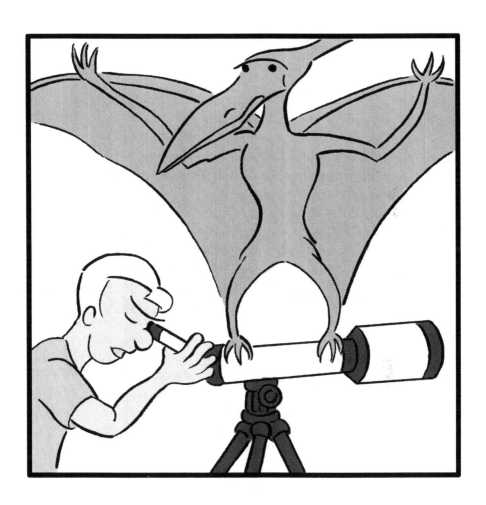

There's nothing to see out there.

Visiting Museums

I told you not to tickle it.

CLAUDE FILION AND DAVID GNASS

Visiting Art Galleries

Quite avant-garde, yet mainstream.

Doing Tai Chi

CLAUDE FILION AND DAVID GNASS

Doing Yoga

Daydreaming

Let's rest on this log for a while.

CLAUDE FILION AND DAVID GNASS

Camping

Kumbaya, my Lord, kumbaya . . .

Cruising

Are you sure you paid for this cruise?

CLAUDE FILION AND DAVID GNASS

Sightseeing

Hike!

2. HOUSEHOLD CHORES

Grooming

Can you smell my cologne?

Dieting

I told you not to eat between meals.

CLAUDE FILION AND DAVID GNASS

Cooking

Is it spicy enough?

Barbecuing

CLAUDE FILION AND DAVID GNASS

Washing Dishes

You wash. I dry.

Sweeping

CLAUDE FILION AND DAVID GNASS

Vacuuming

Have you seen the cat?

House Cleaning

Look what I found in your crate.

CLAUDE FILION AND DAVID GNASS

Chopping Wood

Hiya!

Doing House Repairs

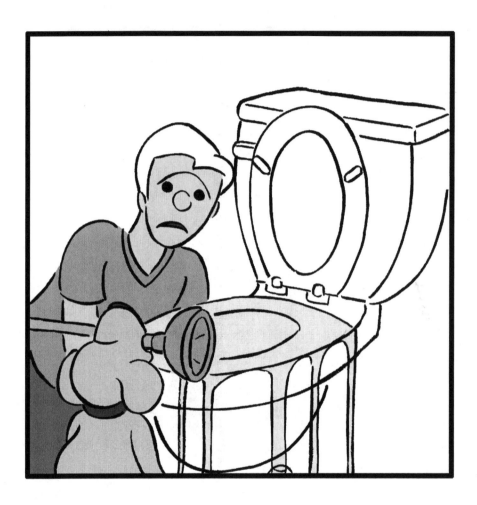

Not now. I'm too busy to play.

CLAUDE FILION AND DAVID GNASS

Working on the Car

By the way, that's molasses, not motor oil.

Investing

CLAUDE FILION AND DAVID GNASS

Mopping

Isn't that my wig?

3. EXERCISE ACTIVITIES

Walking

Do you enjoy our walks as much as I do?

Jogging

CLAUDE FILION AND DAVID GNASS

Rollerblading

Cycling

Did you feel that bump?

CLAUDE FILION AND DAVID GNASS

Freestyle Riding

Skateboarding

Wow. Did you see that trick?

CLAUDE FILION AND DAVID GNASS

Horseback Riding

Take this paper bag with you, in case you get sick.

Playing Frisbee

CLAUDE FILION AND DAVID GNASS

Running on the Treadmill

I think I set the machine too fast.

Exercise Rowing

CLAUDE FILION AND DAVID GNASS

Dancing

Enough. The music stopped five minutes ago.

Canoeing

No. I'm sure it's this way.

CLAUDE FILION AND DAVID GNASS

Hiking

You're not helping me.

Hunting

Did you really go hunting with a paintball gun?

Trapping

So that's how your trap works.

Mountain Climbing

I'll free you in no time.

CLAUDE FILION AND DAVID GNASS

Exploring

I wish I could help you, but it's an endangered species.

Scuba Diving

Can you fetch that pearl for me?

CLAUDE FILION AND DAVID GNASS

Bungee Jumping

Wait!

Skydiving

You forgot your parachute!

CLAUDE FILION AND DAVID GNASS

4. SPORTS ACTIVITIES

Golfing

I suggest you use this club.

Playing Mini Putt

Fore!

CLAUDE FILION AND DAVID GNASS

Playing Tennis

Let!

Bowling

CLAUDE FILION AND DAVID GNASS

Shooting Arrows

Your picture inspires me.

Swimming

Don`t just stand there. Jump in.

Diving

Waterskiing

Look, Ma. No hands.

CLAUDE FILION AND DAVID GNASS

Skiing

Après-Skiing

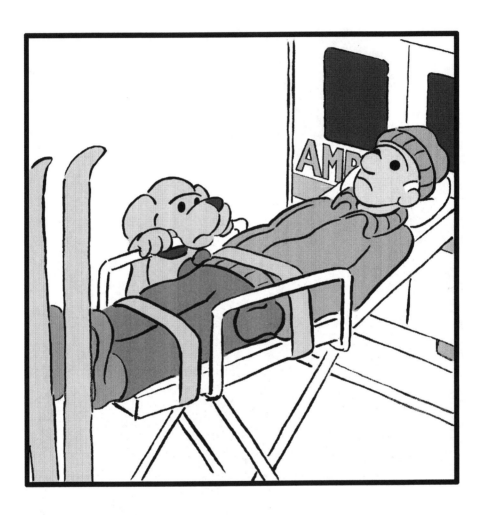

CLAUDE FILION AND DAVID GNASS

Cross-Country Skiing

How did you do that?

Ski Jumping

CLAUDE FILION AND DAVID GNASS

Figure Skating

Once she starts spinning, she can't stop.

Boxing

I won! I won!

Playing Rugby

Soccer

CLAUDE FILION AND DAVID GNASS

5. NEW CAREERS

Agility Instructor

Pet Groomer

I lost your nail clippers.

CLAUDE FILION AND DAVID GNASS

Barber

Please be seated.

Aesthetician

Do you want your face buffed?

CLAUDE FILION AND DAVID GNASS

Gas Attendant

Hands up!

Movers

Why can't you do like me, and carry two boxes?

CLAUDE FILION AND DAVID GNASS

Circus Master

For the last time, jump.

Magician

I hope this book tells me how to put you back together.

CLAUDE FILION AND DAVID GNASS

Lumberjack

Timber!

Park Warden

I see no sign of a bigfoot.

CLAUDE FILION AND DAVID GNASS

Lifeguard

Security Guard

Can't you tell the difference between a life jacket and a bulletproof vest?

CLAUDE FILION AND DAVID GNASS

Real Estate Agent

Electrician

What happens if I touch this wire?

CLAUDE FILION AND DAVID GNASS

Firefighter

Wait your turn. I was here first.

Consultant

CLAUDE FILION AND DAVID GNASS

Acupuncturist

Olé!

Dentist

Open wide.

CLAUDE FILION AND DAVID GNASS

Dental Hygienist

Let me whiten your teeth.

Chiropractor

I give up!

CLAUDE FILION AND DAVID GNASS

Nurse

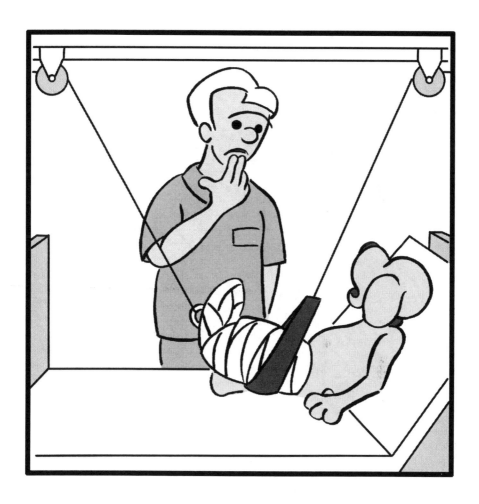

But it's the other leg that hurts.

Surgeon

First, I have to sedate you.

CLAUDE FILION AND DAVID GNASS

Mortician

Maybe you should put the bone back.

Epilog

Remember, it's your retirement. You earned it. Enjoy it. It won't last forever.

What do you want? It's not Halloween.

CLAUDE FILION AND DAVID GNASS

44925074R00068

Made in the USA
Lexington, KY
13 September 2015